D1137981

At **THE DAVID BECKHAM ACADEMY** every day is a footballing adventure. Boys and girls come along to learn about the sport, develop their skills and have fun. But it's not just about tricks and flicks . . . As David Beckham knows, the real secret behind being a Premier League player is understanding the importance of dedication, teamwork, passion and having belief in yourself. In these pages you can meet football-mad children and follow them as they live out their dreams at The Academy.

NORTH EAST LINCOLNSHIRE LIBRARIES

WITHDRAWN FROM STOCK

AUTHORISED:

SO STEP INSIDE AND JOIN THE FUN!

Want to know what some of our readers thought of this book?

'Captain Incredible was an excellent book'
Dominic, age 8

'My favourite character is Dan because
he doesn't give up'
James, age 8

'Kids would definitely enjoy this book
and I love it!'
Abby, age 7

'I liked it when VJ commentated!'
Catriona, age 7

'I like VJ because he is a goal-scoring machine!'
Elliot, age 9

'It's a fantastic book. It teaches you
things like don't be bossy or cheat'
Joshan, age 8

'The pictures were brilliant – they helped
me understand the story'
Rudy Pepe Joy, age 6

'This book is an exciting, humorous
and adventurous story'
Anya, age 7¾

'I liked it when VJ scored a cracking goal!'
George, age 9

ᴊᴘʟ ɪ9-ɪ0

NORTH EAST LINCOLNSHIRE COUNCIL	
00956830	
Bertrams	04/06/2010
	£4.99

First published in Great Britain 2010
by Egmont UK Limited
239 Kensington High Street, London W8 6SA

Text and illustrations © 2010 Beckham Brand Ltd
adidas, Predator, the 3-Bars logo and the 3-Stripes are registered
trademarks of the adidas Group, used with permission

Text by Emily Stead
Cover and inside illustrations by Adam Relf
Cover photography by Anthony Mandler
Designed by Jo Bestall

ISBN 978 1 4052 5165 5

1 3 5 7 9 10 8 6 4 2

A CIP catalogue record for this title is available
from the British Library

Printed and bound in Great Britain by the CPI Group

All rights reserved.

FSC

Mixed Sources
Product group from well-managed
forests and other controlled sources

Cert no. TT-COC-002332
www.fsc.org
© 1996 Forest Stewardship Council

Egmont is passionate about helping to preserve the world's remaining ancient forests.
We only use paper from legal and sustainable forest sources.

This book is made from paper certified by the Forestry Stewardship Council (FSC),
an organisation dedicated to promoting responsible management of forest resources.
For more information on the FSC, please visit www.fsc.org. To learn more about
Egmont's sustainable paper policy, please visit www.egmont.co.uk/ethical

THE DAVID BECKHAM
ACADEMY

CAPTAIN INCREDIBLE

NORTH EAST
LINCOLNSHIRE
LIBRARIES

CLE	LCO
GCL 5/10	NUN
GCR	
GRA	
HUM	WAL
IMM	WIL
LAC	YAR

EGMONT

CONTENTS

ROAD TO THE ACADEMY

Dan Williams sat in the tube-train seat, his hands gripped to the armrests, as the train hurtled through a pitch-black tunnel. Although he knew it wouldn't get them there any quicker, Dan kept his eyes tight shut, willing the train to go faster.

In the seat next to him, his aunt Jess was flicking through the pages of a free newspaper. She had offered it to Dan first, but he couldn't concentrate long enough even to read the football reports at the back. Aunt Jess, he saw, was giving the gossip pages her full attention.

The train whirred to a stop and the doors slid open.

'Please remember to take all personal belongings with you as you leave the train,' came the announcement in a sing-song voice.

'One more stop, one more stop,' said Dan under his breath. His stomach growled

with nerves.

It was his first time on the London Underground, and Dan didn't like it one bit. The dark tunnels, the people almost standing on your toes . . . *It'll be worth it when we get there,* thought Dan.

In the carriage behind, Veejay Ganesh – or VJ as he was known to his friends – and his grandpa were heading for the same destination.

VJ scanned the tube map across from him. A grid of criss-cross coloured lines met his gaze. *Were they nearly there?*

Then came a nudge from Grandpa Ganesh, 'Next stop for The David Beckham Academy!' the old man winked.

VJ sprang up from his seat and stood by the door, ready to jump out the very second the train stopped at the platform.

He had been looking forward to this for *months*. Football was all VJ thought about, from the moment he opened his eyes to the gallery of posters plastered on his bedroom wall in the morning, to when his mum or dad were calling him in at night after hours of keepy-ups practice.

'That football's like your best friend,' his dad would joke. 'You're never apart.'

His 'best friend' sometimes got him into trouble, though. The pair weren't too popular with the neighbours, whose garage doors VJ used for shooting practice.

At school too, VJ would stare out of the window at the football pitches for hours, imagining scoring the goal that would take England to the World Cup and being congratulated by David Beckham and Steven Gerrard.

THWACK! VJ would jerk awake only to find his teacher rapping his textbook on the desk in front of him. Extra maths homework. *Again.*

His grandpa was his biggest fan and never missed any of VJ's matches, not even the friendlies. If the school team were suddenly to announce they were selling season tickets, his grandpa would be first in the queue to buy one.

Even so, Grandpa Ganesh couldn't help teasing his grandson: 'Football's all very well,' he would say, 'but cricket, now there's a *real* sport.'

All that standing around? Rain stopping play? Cricket wasn't for VJ.

The train lurched into the next station and finally stopped. The four passengers got off and soon found themselves being jostled along with the crowd towards the exit.

Dan stared as panels of stainless steel glimmered all around him. He'd known that London would be different to the small village where he lived on his family's farm, but this was nothing like he could have imagined. He felt as though he had been blasted into the future, and was now on board a space station in the year 2075.

His daydream was suddenly interrupted.

'Come on, Grandpa!' It was VJ. He was walking so fast, he had almost broken into a jog. He bounded up the escalator steps two at a time, overtaking Dan and Aunt Jess.

It had taken VJ months to persuade his parents to let him come to The Academy, and he was going to make sure he soaked up every second of his two days there.

'Hang on, these old bones can only go so fast,' Grandpa called with a smile.

VJ turned around to reply, but as he did so, he stumbled and knocked his left ankle on the hard metal step. The handrail broke his fall.

'Careful, VJ,' said his Grandpa, trying to calm his grandson down. 'Let's try to get you there in one piece, shall we?'

'I'm fine, stop fussing,' snapped VJ. He shook out his foot in a bid to stop it hurting. *Ouch.*

From a few steps below, Dan watched the scene. VJ was smaller and slimmer than Dan, and kept his dark hair short and spiky. *That boy must be going to The Academy too,* Dan thought, *I wonder if he's any good.*

As the escalator took them back to ground level, Dan breathed a deep sigh.

Daylight!

The ticket barriers opened, and the boys, Grandpa and Aunt Jess left the station. They crossed the road to be greeted by the huge arches of The Academy.

'Blimey! This place is massive!' gasped VJ. 'Look at it, Grandpa!'

Dan's jaw hung wide open. He felt his heart begin to beat faster in his chest and the hairs on the back of his neck stand on end.

It was so big you could have fitted the whole of the Williams family's farm in it. Welcome to The David Beckham Academy.

WARMING UP

Inside the reception, a small crowd had gathered. There was a buzz of excitement in the air as the smart royal blue Academy kits were handed out. VJ and his grandpa exchanged amazed glances – wait until the rest of the school team saw this strip, everyone would want to swap shirts!

It was soon time for the adults to say goodbye. Grandpa Ganesh held open the glass door for Aunt Jess with one hand, and waved to VJ with the other. 'Enjoy yourself!'

'Score a try for me!' Jess called to Dan.

'That's rugby, Aunt Jess!' said Dan, his ears turning pink. 'Even you know that, *surely*?'

'I mean, er, try not to get out?' said Jess hopefully. *Wrong again.*

'Ah! A cricket fan, I see!' said Grandpa Ganesh gallantly trying to spare Aunt Jess's blushes. 'Let me tell you about the time I watched India beat England for the first time . . .'

VJ shuffled into the queue next to Dan. He could see that Dan looked nervous. Or maybe he was just embarrassed by the strange woman who'd dropped him off. She didn't act like she was his mum, his auntie maybe?

'Hey, wanna see something cool?' said VJ, pulling out a phone from his pocket.

'This is my record keepy-ups attempt – two hundred and seventy-nine!'

Dan squinted at the bright mobile phone display.

'I'm Veejay,' said VJ, without looking away from the screen. 'It would have been way more but my grandpa had to go in cos the cricket was about to start. He's as crazy about cricket as I am about football!'

'Dan,' Dan nodded back. He wasn't going to own up that he couldn't even do ten keepy-ups. 'Speaking of crazy,' he blurted out, trying to change the subject. 'I, er, won a competition in *Football Crazy* magazine to come here.'

'Oh, yeah?' VJ replied. He sounded impressed. 'I get that magazine every week!'

'Yeah, you had to send in a photo of "the strangest place you've ever played football" . . . mine was one of me and my sister on our farm, in a field full of cows. We said we were playing the Juventus B team!' Dan went on.

'Ha!' laughed VJ. 'The famous black and whites! That's pretty funny!'

As they were coming to the end of the video clip, a girl with black bobbed hair barged past them and straight to the front of the queue. She almost knocked the phone out of VJ's hand.

'Hey, watch where you're –' VJ began, but the girl wasn't listening.

'I'm Mia,' they heard her announce as she held out a hand to the coach. 'Captain of Wallingworth Under-Elevens. Last season I scored eight goals and played in every single match.'

Mia held up a pink notebook with a football sticker on the cover. 'I write down all the scores and match reports in this notebook, see. My dad says I could make the Olympic women's team the rate I'm going!' she beamed.

VJ rolled his eyes. 'I hope I'm not in the same team as *her*. Does she ever stop talking?'

The coach winked at Dan, and Dan

smiled back.

'OK, everyone, I'm Woody and I'm going to be your coach for the next few days,' he explained. 'I want you changed and on the pitch in five minutes, ready for the warm-up.'

VJ, Dan and the others didn't need telling twice, and headed straight for the changing rooms.

● ● ●

Twenty minutes later, the warm-up was over and the teams were decided for the skills session. Dan and VJ were together with another curly-haired boy called Jack.

The first exercise was a three-on-three mini game, where the teams had to stay inside a small square marked out with cones.

'This is about teamwork and keeping

possession of the ball,' said Woody. 'I want to see you working together and choosing the best pass. There aren't any goals, so just keep hold of the ball for as long as you can.'

They were up against Mia's team. Mia was guarding the ball under one arm and telling her teammates exactly what they should and shouldn't do — as if it were their first time playing football!

'Just my luck!' moaned VJ.

Woody blew the whistle to signal the start of the exercise. The smaller boy on Mia's team kicked off.

'Over here,' called Mia. 'I'm free!'

But Dan had spotted the danger, and easily cut out the pass.

'Too slow!' Mia groaned.

Dan squared the ball neatly to VJ, who faked to go one way, then passed the ball the other, to Jack.

'Close him down, why don't you!' Mia shrieked.

While VJ's team quickly got into the habit of running into space to receive the ball and choosing easy passes, Mia put pressure on her teammates to pass to her every time – even if she was being marked.

By the time the whistle blew again, it was VJ's team who had kept the ball for almost the whole time.

'Great stuff, guys!' said Woody, clapping his hands briskly.

'That was a stupid exercise anyway,' huffed Mia, pulling off her bib. 'You'd have loads more space to pass the ball in a real game.'

Dan frowned. *That wasn't the point and she knew it.* He said nothing. The last thing he wanted was to get into an argument.

Mia snatched a drink from the water bottle carrier and squeezed a long flow of water into her mouth.

VJ and Dan glanced at each other with the same thought going through their head. *Nightmare*.

'Right, everyone,' smiled Woody. 'I hope you lot have been working on your samba skills, as you're *all* in Team Brazil today!'

The whole group was delighted. But their faces dropped they saw Mia pulling on a yellow Brazil bib.

'Has everyone got a bib?' she asked bossily.

WORLD CUP FEVER

'This is going to be wicked,' smiled VJ, bending to check his laces were tied for what was the third time that minute. In the break, Woody had told Team Brazil that their first opponents were Japan.

The chatter in the boys' changing room as they took a quick break was of famous countries and World Cup wonder goals.

They agreed that playing as Brazil would do their chances no harm at all. No team had been World Champions more times than Brazil – they were one of the strongest football nations in the world.

'Let's just hope that England don't draw Brazil in the real World Cup!' said one boy.

'Just imagine all those amazing countries and legendary stadiums that David Beckham has played in,' said VJ as they swung out of the changing room. 'It's unreal to think that he's played over a hundred times for England.'

Dan opened his mouth to reply.

'Try more like one hundred and twenty,' Mia butted in.

'There's nothing like having a *private* conversation, eh, Danny boy?' VJ said, loud enough for Mia to hear.

Mia chose to ignore him. 'So Team, we should treat this like a real World Cup: be confident and patient, and the goals will come,' she went on, checking her captain's

armband was not about to slip down her arm.

The rest of the team shrugged. What Mia said made sense. But when was it decided that she would be captain?

● ● ●

Mia was proven right. Team Brazil settled into the match as though they had been playing together for years.

They calmly made slick passes and put in sensible tackles, with everyone helping to defend when the opposition tried to push up.

VJ's skills did not let him down either. His best bit of play was when he managed to round four defenders and beat the keeper with a low drive into the corner of the goal to open the scoring. It was as though the ball was tied to his foot with a piece of elastic!

And the celebration was even better, as VJ sprinted the length of the pitch adding a forward flip before collapsing happily in a heap. As his teammates rushed over to congratulate him Veejay didn't have time to worry about the twinge he felt in his ankle.

No one added to the score sheet until midway into the second half, when VJ made the most of some sloppy defending. Latching on to a pass from Dan, he burst into the box to set up Mia with an easy tap-in.

'That's how it's done!' beamed Mia, picking the ball out of the net.

In defence, Dan and the full-backs looked solid too. The only danger came late on when a Japan striker could only scuff his shot straight at the grateful keeper.

With five minutes to go, the game was all but won. The 2–0 final score actually flattered Japan – they had never really tested the Brazil goal, while at the other end Team Japan's keeper had made a string of fine saves.

Keen to seal the win, VJ scampered off on a run. A Japan defender bore down on him, but VJ cleverly knocked the ball through his legs. Nutmeg! Embarrassed, the defender desperately stuck out a foot and made contact . . . directly with VJ's ankle.

'That's got to hurt!' exclaimed Mia.

Dan winced. *Helpful as ever, Mia,* he thought. He went over to help VJ to his feet.

'Play on, ref,' said VJ, getting up gingerly. 'I'm all right.'

Dan shot VJ a look to say, 'Are you really

OK?' but VJ looked straight past him and placed the ball ready to take the free kick.

VJ stood for a moment with his hands on hips, before wasting the opportunity. The goalkeeper smothered his soft shot comfortably. So much for a third goal.

The last few minutes saw VJ grimace with every kick of the ball. The full-time whistle couldn't come quickly enough for him.

When the ref finally blew for time, Dan caught up with VJ, who was heading off the pitch, hobbling slightly.

'That was a pretty bad challenge. Are you sure your foot's OK?' asked Dan in a concerned voice.

'I've got another one!' VJ said, jokingly. 'Good job I'm not right-footed, eh?'

Dan's brow furrowed.

'Seriously, don't sweat about me, mate,' VJ replied. He could see that Dan was worried.

On the next pitch, another game was still going on. South Africa were thrashing Spain, and seemed to score with every attack they went on.

Dan and VJ watched in amazement as the South African captain rifled a thunderous volley into the back of the net.

'Now there's something to *really* worry about,' said VJ solemnly.

INJURY TIME

When Woody announced it was lunchtime, everyone had suddenly felt very hungry. Something good was cooking in the canteen.

As usual, Mia was first in line.

'Chicken for protein, vegetables for vitamins and pasta for carbohydrates to give you energy,' said Mia.

'That's right, dear,' said the serving lady. 'Just like the professionals eat.'

Dan and VJ were dawdling at the back, studying the plaque on one of Beckham's framed England shirts. Last to get their food, they found the only two free seats left were next to Mia.

'She *is* on our team,' Dan shrugged.

'After you,' smiled VJ.

'Have you heard?' said Mia, when they had sat down. 'We're playing Argentina in the next round.'

'Wicked! A South American derby,' VJ declared. Putting on his best football-commentator's voice, he continued. 'Brazil face their toughest test yet, against bitter rivals, Argentina.'

Dan half-laughed and half-choked on his baked potato.

'Hell-ooo! Can you stop messing around, please, VJ?' said Mia, bossily. 'We have to win this match.'

First though, the teams were gathered for some time out in the classroom. VJ was glad to take the weight off his ankle.

They were given the task of designing a newspaper page, and had to write a match report all about the game they had played that morning.

Much to VJ's dismay, he found himself in Mia's group again. At least he had Dan for company.

'I want to see some really lively headlines,' said Woody as the groups busied themselves with pieces of paper and markers. 'Think of something that's going to grab people's attention.'

The next thirty minutes passed without incident. Everyone seemed to have their heads down, getting on with the report.

When Woody indicated to the class that their time was just about up, each group huddled to quickly finish their designs.

'Dan, tell us how your team got on, please,' smiled Woody warmly. 'Let's hear your headline.'

Dan felt queasy. He had the same sick feeling as he sometimes got at school when the teachers asked him to do something in front of the whole class.

He had actually enjoyed the activity and had helped to draw the lettering for the headline. Small group stuff he was fine with, but talking in front of all these people? Sweat began to bead on his top lip.

Some of the others were still chattering. But Dan wasn't. His eyes were fixed on the paper in front of him, trying to avoid Woody's gaze.

Then . . .

'Excuse me, coach —' came a voice from the other side of the table. It was VJ.

Dan felt a rush of relief.

'Thank you, VJ,' said Woody. 'If you want to volunteer to read, then —'

'Actually — I — er, was just going to ask if I could go to the toilet,' said VJ.

A groan of disgust came from Mia. 'I might have known I'd have to do it myself,' she said, snatching the paper from Dan.

Dan flashed VJ a smile. Panic over.

'BRAZIL KICK OFF CAMPAIGN IN STYLE...' Mia read confidently as VJ slipped out of the room.

He hobbled down the corridor, each step hurting more than the last. Once inside the boys' toilets, he pushed open the three cubicle doors in turn. When he saw that he was completely alone, he let out a long, low sigh.

Grabbing a handful of paper towels from the dispenser, VJ ran them under the cold tap. The towels quickly soaked through and VJ squeezed out the excess water. He sat on the floor to roll down his sock.

VJ could already see that his ankle looked bad. Bright red, it had ballooned to twice the size of his right ankle. He loosened his

laces and pressed the wet towels on to the swelling. The cool sensation felt soothing.

Slowly, he got to his feet. VJ caught sight of his own reflection in the mirror for a second and a pale face stared back. 'There's no way I'm going to miss playing in the South American derby!' he said aloud.

He returned to find the classroom empty. The lesson was over and it was almost time for kick-off.

VJ headed back to the pitches.

'Ah, VJ,' Mia sneered. 'Nice of you to join us.'

● ● ●

The match began much as the previous one had. Dan put in some expertly timed tackles, while VJ led the line in attack.

Each player had a job to do, and was doing it well.

Dan was playing out of his skin. Not one attacker had managed to get past him, which gave Brazil the confidence to hold on to the ball without panicking.

Midway through the second half, Dan collected a harmless shot that had ended up closer to the corner flag than the actual goal. Then there was trouble.

Mia called for the ball in front of the

Brazil goal. 'Pass it to me, *now!*' she demanded.

'Down the line – I'm free,' called another player, who was hugging the touchline.

'To *me!*' Mia screeched again.

Confused, Dan played a short pass to Mia. But rather than coming to meet the ball, she didn't move a muscle, except for the ones in her mouth, as she continued to shriek loudly.

A short, skilful boy on Team Argentina spotted his chance. He stuck out a foot to intercept the pass, then nipped ahead of Mia.

Dan covered his face with both hands as the striker poked the ball past the keeper.

Mia was purple with rage. She spun around and glared at Dan. 'Well that was all your fault, *obviously.*'

Dan felt a lump begin to rise in his throat. Why wouldn't any words come out? Why wouldn't his mouth let him defend himself?

'I'm your captain. Try not to show me up, will you?' Mia continued in a sour tone.

VJ cut in quickly. 'Yeah, well who made you captain, anyway?' he scowled, leaping to Dan's defence. 'It's not like any of us actually *wanted* you to be our skipper.'

As soon as he'd said the words, VJ knew they had sounded harsher than he had meant, but he didn't apologise. He couldn't believe anyone could be so interfering.

The three trudged back to their positions in silence.

VJ took the kick-off. Determined to even up the scores, he set off on a mazy run. A stocky Argentina defender closed him down. He was right on his shoulder.

VJ released the ball to Mia, who played it ahead into space for VJ to run on to. There was just one defender between VJ and the penalty box.

Beat him and I'm in on goal, the thought flew into VJ's head. Looking up, he tried a step-over, but he planted his foot back down on the ground awkwardly. His ankle gave way and VJ hit the turf in a fit of terrible pain.

LESSON LEARNED

Five minutes later, VJ was lying on a bed in the physio room. His ankle was bound tightly, with an ice pack underneath to reduce the swelling.

The two physios were making their assessment. 'There's no ligament damage, luckily,' said a tall man wearing an Academy tracksuit.

The other, blond man looked younger. Not that much older than some of the bigger kids at The Academy, in fact. He had the same tracksuit on, with the initials 'MS' on the chest. VJ watched as he scribbled notes on a clipboard.

Mark Seal, physiotherapist, VJ read.

He turned to VJ. 'Your ankle,' he said in a matter-of-fact voice. 'This didn't happen just now, did it?'

'It – er,' spluttered VJ. He suddenly remembered the paper towels he had stuffed down his socks, and wished the room would swallow him up.

'Look, if you get injured, you've *got* to tell your coach straight away,' the physio said softly. 'If you play on when you're carrying an injury, you could make it a lot worse. Don't make the same mistake that I did.'

VJ propped himself up on his elbows. 'What happened to you?'

'I'd been in the youth team at West Ham since I was twelve. I trained hard, ate healthily, and always made sure I got enough sleep. I'd just turned seventeen and was playing well. Then one day, I finally got the nod from the gaffer to make my first team debut.'

VJ imagined the scene in his head. A packed Upton Park stadium, just down the road from his own house . . . The floodlights beaming down, the Premier

League cameras . . .

'Ten minutes in, I was dribbling with the ball – no one near me – when I slipped. My right knee twisted and made this weird sound. I knew it didn't feel right, but I was desperate to play on. The very next move, I was collecting a pass when a defender slid in with his studs up. My knee just went. And that was it. Stretchered off and straight to hospital.'

VJ pictured the tackle, and winced at the image of the physio's leg buckling under him.

'They tried surgery to fix it, but my knee just wasn't strong enough. I haven't been able to play anything more than a quick kick-about since.'

VJ's eyes widened. 'Was it your cruciate ligament?'

Mark nodded his head, impressed by VJ. 'It was.'

'I read in a magazine that it's the most feared injury in football,' said VJ, his cheeks reddening.

'It wasn't the end of the world. I'm lucky, really,' Mark continued as he turned to wash his hands in the basin.

'Lucky?' exclaimed VJ. 'How do you work that out?'

Mark told VJ all about how he had had his studies to fall back on when he'd been forced to hang up his boots. About how he'd trained to be a physio and about the work he did at The Academy.

'So now I still get to work in football. And when players get injured, I help them to get back on the pitch as quickly as possible. It's a good feeling, I can tell you,'

Mark said.

VJ went quiet for a moment, and began to think about his own studies. Maybe he should pay more attention at school, after all.

● ● ●

Grandpa Ganesh came to collect VJ early, in the car this time.

'You should have seen it, Grandpa,' said

VJ from the passenger seat, as they drove away from The Academy. 'There was no way I wouldn't have scored if my stupid ankle hadn't let me down. The keeper was well off his line.'

Grandpa smiled, but kept his eyes on the road.

'At first everyone thought I'd broken it, but then Mark the physio checked me over,' VJ went on without pausing for breath. 'He said it's just a sprain but it feels nearly broken.'

'Nearly broken, eh?' said Grandpa Ganesh, raising an eyebrow. 'It doesn't sound like you'll be going back tomorrow then.'

'No, wait!' cried VJ. 'I didn't mean –'

'Mark said you just need to rest it,' said Grandpa soothingly. 'We'll see how you feel in the morning.'

VJ went quiet. He listened to the clicking of the indicator. His face looked pale. Worried. As the lights changed, they moved off.

'I would never have thought you'd throw in the towel so easily,' said Grandpa after a few moments of rare silence. 'What if David Beckham had given up when he had that sore toe just before the last World Cup? He would have missed the whole tournament.'

'Grandpa!' scoffed VJ. 'It was more than just a sore toe – he broke a metatarsal bone. I bet it was agony!'

'Well, your meta-whatsits are all still working, aren't they?' Grandpa smiled.

It suddenly dawned on VJ that he was maybe being a bit dramatic about his own injury – it was a just knock on the ankle, after all. He made up his mind to stop complaining about it there and then.

FOUL PLAY

Early the next day, the physio team checked VJ's ankle. Surprisingly, the swelling had gone down and the only mark left behind was a small, purplish bruise.

'I feel one hundred per cent,' said VJ, in the most convincing voice he could manage. His heart, though, was racing in his chest. What if his ankle started hurting again? What if he could only *watch* the semi-final?

The physios weren't taking any chances. Mark warmed VJ up at the side of one of the pitches. Some light running to begin with, then on to some ball work, before finishing with a few sprints.

Much to VJ's relief, his ankle passed the test. He jogged over to join the others as the team talk was just beginning.

Woody had gathered Brazil into a huddle. 'Yesterday's match,' he started. 'The way you played for each other was excellent. When you went 1–0 down, you didn't let your heads drop. OK, so the winning goal may have been a lucky deflection, but you kept on going. You deserved to beat Argentina.'

He warned them about their next opponents. Brazil would have to put in another top performance if they were going to beat Mexico.

The quarter-final was a tense affair. Brazil

began nervously, mostly keeping the ball in their own half. Mexico were a tough side to break down, and they didn't seem in a hurry to score.

Eleven minutes in, though, disaster struck. Mexico broke the deadlock with a shot that rebounded off the crossbar. The confused Brazil keeper swung round, to see

the ball land at the feet of a pony-tailed striker, who slotted it home for Mexico.

'One–nil!' sang the team in green bibs as they lined up to perform a Mexican wave.

Mia was fuming! 'Let's see if you're still singing at the end,' she huffed, snatching the ball from the Mexico captain.

A change of ends at half-time did little to improve Brazil's fortunes. Mia and her team were putting in as much effort as they did every match, but the ball just wasn't falling kindly for them.

Mia knew why it was happening. It was often the way in semi-finals. She'd seen matches on TV just like this one. Brazil hadn't scored because they were nervous. No one was willing to take a risk and go on the attack in case they gave the ball away.

There was so much at stake, so much to lose. But the only way to score *was* to attack — they had to create a chance to score.

All we need is one slice of luck to put us back on level terms, Mia thought. *One chance.* But was luck on Mexico's side today? She had to do something, she decided.

A minute later Mia called for the ball and Dan passed it straight to her feet. She knocked it past a lanky midfielder with a good first touch, and ran on to collect it.

Ahead of her, another girl playing for Mexico was arriving in full flow. It was a fifty-fifty ball, the quickest player to get to the ball would win it . . .

The challenge, though a little clumsy, was a fair one. As the ball was cleared safely away, the defender's trailing leg accidentally clipped Mia's heel. Mia tumbled to the ground in spectacular fashion.

The referee's arms stayed firmly by his sides. There was no whistle, and no free kick was awarded.

'Play on!' Dan called to encourage his team.

Suddenly, something snapped in Mia's head. The defender had barely touched her, but you wouldn't have known that from the way she was rolling on the floor. It was as though she had been bitten by a snake!

The ref wasn't fooled. He had seen the tackle clearly. Mia was pretending to be hurt. He walked over to where she was kneeling, and took out something from his top pocket. *It was a red card!*

'Stand on the sidelines until the match has finished, please, Mia,' said the ref without raising his voice.

Everyone stood in shocked silence while Mia got to her feet.

'Mia,' VJ whispered as she approached him, and nodded at her captain's armband. She had to give it to someone else on their team.

But instead of handing it over calmly, Mia hurled it to the ground. She ran off

down the tunnel without looking back.

For the next few seconds no one moved. Their eyes were fixed on the armband.

VJ, who couldn't bear long silences, tossed it to Dan and grinned. 'What are you waiting for? Put it on!'

Dan stared in disbelief. 'You – sure?' he stuttered.

'Positive! Now come on, we've got a match to win,' said VJ.

The rest of the team nodded their approval.

If he had stopped to think about it for more than a second, Dan would have changed his mind. Captain of Brazil at The David Beckham Academy? He would have been terrified. But instead, he pulled on the armband and jogged back into position.

Ten minutes later, Mia reappeared.

The game was still going on, just without her in it. Although they were a man down and there was more work to get through, Brazil looked settled.

Mia trained her eyes on Dan, like a camera following his every move. He looked calm, assured, she noticed. And when he called instructions to his teammates, he didn't shout and they didn't ignore him. The opposite of the way she had behaved.

Mia couldn't help but think that being captain suited Dan. The quiet one, the gentle giant. He had won the team's respect without even trying.

As the match carried on, there was an urgency in Brazil's play. They were looking stronger with every move. The fight-back was on.

Dan cleared a long ball to a teammate

in the opposition half, who shrugged off
a tackle and released the ball to VJ. This was
their chance, and VJ was not about to fluff
it. Cool as you like, he fired a crisp shot into
the top corner of the goal.

'Yes!' shouted VJ, punching the air. No
fancy goal celebration this time.

'Reset quickly, guys,' urged Dan, clapping
his hands. 'We're into added time.'

On the sidelines, the effects of Mia's
sending-off were sinking in. She knew she
had gone too far this time. If only she'd kept
her cool, she'd still be on the pitch, helping
her teammates. Her eyes became watery
and a single tear rolled down her cheek.

Then something incredible happened
. . . The play broke quickly for Brazil to
counter-attack . . . The keeper threw the ball
out to Dan, who tapped it to the full-back,

who threaded a neat ball to the central midfielder . . . He in turn crossed to VJ on the left wing, who passed it back, before the left-back sprayed a pass across the field and into the box. The Brazil striker was clean through, and a simple side-foot shot was enough to make the scoreline 2–1.

'You're not waving, you're not waving, you're not waving any more!' VJ sang cheekily to the opposition.

'You're not waving any more!' the rest of Team Brazil joined in.

Even Mia's expression changed! The corners of her lips curled slightly into what looked suspiciously like a smile.

Seconds later, the full-time whistle blew. They had done it. They were in the final!

THE PROMOTION

After a much-needed drinks break, lunch was served. The canteen was buzzing with excitement. Dan and VJ couldn't help grinning at each other as the team discussed their next game.

South Africa were Brazil's next and final opponents in the match that would decide the winners of the champions' trophy.

As he stood up to clear away his tray, VJ caught sight of Mia and Woody on the next table, deep in conversation. He couldn't quite hear what was being said, but Mia certainly looked sorry for herself. Would she do it . . . would she swallow her pride? VJ wasn't convinced.

Mia got to her feet. Red-faced, she turned to face the table where Brazil were sitting. 'I'm sorry I let you down,' she said in a small voice. 'I'll understand if you don't want me on the team for the final.'

No one quite knew what to say. Dan heard whispers behind him as Mia stared at him, looking helpless. 'Course we want you on the team,' he said. 'We need you just as much as we need any other player.'

It was decided that Dan would captain the side against South Africa. Woody had been pleased with the way Dan had led his team from the jaws of defeat against Mexico and told him to hang on to the

captain's armband.

The build up to the final was unbelievable. As the match drew closer, the players were noticeably jittery, not least their captain. Dan felt a mix of nerves and excitement in the pit of his stomach.

VJ tried to lighten the mood with the football-commentator impression that he'd begun to call on whenever he recognised Dan's serious face. But Dan wasn't listening, he was completely focused on the match.

With a shrug of his shoulders, VJ decided to give Dan some peace and turned to leave the changing rooms.

'I'll catch you up in a second,' Dan called after him.

But the second turned into a minute, and one minute turned into five. When their captain didn't show up on the pitch, Brazil began to worry.

'Has anyone seen Dan?' asked Woody.

VJ made a face in apology. 'I thought he was right behind me.'

'Practise some penalties until I get back,' said Woody, tossing a whistle to the assistant coach.

Moments later, Woody swung open the doors to the corridor to find Dan sitting

quietly with his back against the wall. 'Everything OK, Dan?'

'Sorry, coach,' Dan replied, getting to his feet. 'I just needed a minute.' He didn't want Woody to think he wasn't grateful for making him captain.

He had his hand on the door, about to push it open when he stopped, making Woody stop too.

For a few seconds, there was silence. Then Woody said, 'Before we go back on the pitch, is there anything you want to get anything off your chest?'

Dan nodded. But the words wouldn't come.

'When *I* first came here to The Academy as a coach I was so nervous,' Woody said kindly. 'All sorts of things were going through my head. Would people like me? Would I be a good coach? Should I just have carried on working in my dad's shop?

'Then I remembered my job interview, when I first met David Beckham. "Believe in yourself," he said to me. And that's what I started to do.'

He smiled at Dan broadly. 'I chose you to be captain because you're a special kid. You've got everything a coach could ever want in a captain – your bravery, your hunger, the positive influence you have on your teammates . . . The team spirit in that second half was incredible – thanks to you.'

Dan blushed. He had never heard anyone say so many nice things about him in one go before. He wouldn't let it go to his head, but it felt good hearing the coach's words. With that, Dan strode on to the pitch. Game on.

LIKE WATCHING BRAZIL

The final kicked off with a nail-biting opening period. South Africa lived up to their billing as the tournament's team to beat. They had managed five shots on goal with only seven minutes played.

Aunt Jess and the other parents were watching from the sidelines. Next to Jess stood Grandpa Ganesh.

'Come on, we can do this,' Dan called to his teammates. His chest heaved, heavy with emotion. He knew how well the team could perform and didn't doubt for one second that they wouldn't win the match.

With a burst of speed, VJ flew past a defender and struck a clinical shot beyond the keeper. The players went wild.

'That's my boy!' cheered his grandpa.

There was soon cause for more celebrations when Mia netted a second for Brazil. Her face beamed with pleasure.

Too quickly though, their bubble burst. South Africa put together a slick move, which ended with a goal that was simply unstoppable. For how long could Brazil hold on to their 2–1 lead?

To their credit, they didn't give up. Then in the dying seconds of the game, the ref awarded Brazil a corner kick.

Dan quickly gathered the team into a huddle. 'OK, here's what I want us to try . . .' he began. 'Mia will take the corner and –'

'But I always take the corners,' VJ protested. 'Come on, mate!'

'Let me finish,' Dan said firmly. 'I need you in the box. I want you to use your speed and make a run at the last minute. That way you'll draw your defender and hopefully create some space for me to try to score.'

His teammates nodded their agreement.

Dan's plan might just work, they thought.

Mia swung in a weary corner and watched the ball loop high above the South Africa defenders. Dan met the cross with a terrific leap and fired a bullet header into the back of the net. The plan had worked perfectly – *Goooaaall!*

Anyone passing outside The Academy might well have thought some sort of demolition work was taking place, so loud was the noise that erupted from Dan's teammates.

'Ha, ha! It's just like watching Brazil!' smiled Grandpa, hopping from foot to foot.

Aunt Jess scratched her head. 'Excuse me,' she said. 'But I thought we *were* watching Brazil.'

The whistle blew and that was it. Brazil were crowned the tournament champions.

The medal ceremony followed, with Dan leading his team to collect the trophy. He raised the cup in the air as a great roar of applause broke out.

'Let's hear it for our skipper . . .' laughed VJ. 'CAPTAIN INCREDIBLE!'

There was another deafening cheer.

Too soon, it was time to leave The Academy. Dan hung back to say goodbye to VJ.

'See you, then,' he mumbled.

'You bet,' smiled VJ. 'Text your mum and dad and ask them if I can come and stay this summer. We can watch the World Cup together!'

Dan studied his friend. Why on earth would VJ want to come and stay in the middle of nowhere?

Then VJ spoke as if he were reading Dan's

mind. 'All those fields . . . you've got your very own private pitch!' he smiled, his eyes wide. 'And I've got to be a better teammate than a cow, right?'

'Come on, you two,' said Aunt Jess, fiddling with the buttons on her camera phone. 'This photo will be worth a fortune when you're famous footballers!'

As he smiled for the photograph, Dan had never felt more proud. The last two days

really had been *incredible*. Now that he knew he could be a captain, he felt like anything was possible.

HAVE YOU READ

AWAY FROM HOME

THE FIFTH BOOK IN THE DAVID BECKHAM ACADEMY SERIES?

TURN THE PAGE TO READ A SNEAK PREVIEW!

GOING DUTCH

George polished his glasses and put them back on.

'I don't get it. If we're Holland, why don't we get orange kits?'

Ben sighed as he pulled the blue David Beckham Academy football shirt over his head.

'Look, we're not *really* Holland,' he explained for the second time. 'That's just a name for our team. That lot over there are France. And I know they're not French because three of them go to my school!'

'So we aren't going to have a Dutch coach then?' George asked.

'No,' said Ben patiently. 'We'll have an English coach. We're just *called* Holland.'

George seemed to get the message at last and bent down to lace up his football boots. 'Well, I don't see why they have to make it so confusing!' he muttered.

Ben was about to suggest that it was actually quite simple when three more boys shoved their way through the huddle in the boys' changing room.

'Are you lot Holland?' asked a tall boy with scruffy brown hair.

'Yep!' nodded Ben. 'Welcome to the team! I'm Ben and this is George.'

The team members quickly introduced themselves and pulled on their new football kits.

'So who's your favourite player?' asked George, smoothing down his ginger hair in a nearby mirror.

'David Beckham, of course!' said Ben, checking his own crop of curly black hair in the mirror. 'What about you?'

Within minutes, all the members of the Holland team were arguing about their favourite players and boasting about how

they were *definitely* going to be the best team at The Academy.

'I'm telling you guys, we *have* to win!' cried Ben.

'Yeah!' cried George. 'How about we pick our positions before the coach gets here? I play on the left wing!'

'I'm a midfielder,' said Ben.

'I play in midfield too!' said another boy.

'What about you?' said George, to a short boy with dark, spiky hair who had just joined the group. 'What's your favourite position?'

The boy looked blankly at George and didn't answer.

'Hey!' said Ben, assuming the boy hadn't heard. 'You're in Holland, right? What's your name?'

The boy looked blank again and

shrugged nervously.

'You must know your name!' said Ben. 'What are you called?'

The boy's face suddenly lit up. 'Stefan!' he said in a foreign accent.

'Aha!' said George. 'I knew it! A Dutchman!'

Ben rolled his eyes. 'Will you shut up about Dutchmen? I've told you . . .'

But George was questioning Stefan in a slow, loud voice.

'Are . . . you . . . from . . . Holland?' he asked, mouthing the words as he spoke. Stefan just shrugged again.

'Do . . . you . . . speak . . . English?' George continued.

Stefan seemed to understand and shook his head. 'No English,' he said.

George looked smugly at Ben. 'See!' he

said. 'He's not English. He's *definitely* from Holland!'

Ben groaned. 'Just because he's foreign, doesn't mean he's Dutch!' he replied with a sigh. 'He doesn't even have a Dutch accent!'

Stefan seemed to realise they were talking about him and started to blush. He began fidgeting with a pile of football stickers in his shorts pocket.

'So what kind of accent *does* he have, then?' asked George.

Ben hesitated. 'Well, it's obvious, isn't it?' he began, uncertainly, but he didn't add anything more.

Before George could quiz Ben further, Stefan took the stickers from his pocket and began shuffling through them. The other boys gathered round, studying each sticker as it was flicked from the top to the bottom of the pack.

Names flashed by in a blur – Jodlowiec, Komorowski, Boruc – each name as unfamiliar as the one before.

George called out excitedly as a shiny foil sticker caught his eye. 'Hey, that's the Polish flag! It was the very last sticker I swapped to finish my album,' he announced. 'Poland have finished third in two World Cups – 1974 and 1982, you know.'

Ben laughed. 'Someone knows their stats!'

'So Stefan, that means you're from Poland, right?' asked George.

'Polska!' nodded Stefan, feeling encouraged.

'Mystery solved,' smiled Ben. He reached into his own pocket and took out a pile of stickers held together in an elastic band. Holding them out to Stefan, he asked, 'Know any of these guys?'

Stefan frowned and shook his head at the first few footballers in Ben's collection. He knew quite a few of the famous players at British clubs, but the faces on these stickers were as unfamiliar to him as the Polish players had been to the other boys.

'How about this one?' said Ben, stopping

halfway through the pack. He held up the most prized of all his stickers. 'You must have heard of him!'

'BECK-HAM!' smiled Stefan, giving Ben the thumbs-up.

'That's right!' replied Ben, approvingly. 'David Beckham.'

'I'd be surprised if you didn't know who Beckham was,' laughed George. 'We are at his Academy, after all!'

The boys were still comparing stickers when a tallish woman in a smart Academy tracksuit knocked on the changing room door. 'I'm Kelly, your coach for the next few days,' she addressed the team. 'Ready for training, Holland?'

'You bet!' cried George, excitedly. He waited until Kelly had left before whispering to Ben, 'Holland. That's us, right?'

'*Yes!*' laughed Ben, leading the other boys out into the corridor. 'Now let's go get us some goals.'

Collect all the books in
The David Beckham Academy range

● ● ● ● ● ● ● ● ● ● ● ● ●

STORY BOOKS

1. Twin Trouble	ISBN 978 1 4052 4524 1	£4.99
2. Le Football	ISBN 978 1 4052 4525 8	£4.99
3. Save the Day	ISBN 978 1 4052 4526 5	£4.99
4. Bossy Boots	ISBN 978 1 4052 4527 2	£4.99
5. Away From Home	ISBN 978 1 4052 5164 8	£4.99
6. Captain Incredible	ISBN 978 1 4052 5165 5	£4.99

ACTIVITY BOOKS

How-to Handbook	ISBN 978 1 4052 4669 9	£4.99
Ultimate Football Sticker Book	ISBN 978 1 4052 4670 5	£4.99
Champion Cards Activity Book	ISBN 978 1 4052 5121 1	£4.99

● ● ● ● ● ● ● ● ● ● ● ● ●

WIN!

SIGNED DAVID BECKHAM ACADEMY BOOKS

We're giving away 25 copies of the action-packed footy story **Twin Trouble**, signed by David Beckham himself.*

PLUS! More books to collect...

Simply visit
www.egmont.co.uk/academy

*Terms and conditions apply. See online for full details.

E0601